REBELS WITH A VERY GOOD CAUSE

SUFFOLK STORIES FOR YOUNG ADVENTURERS

Rebels With a Very Good Cause

Published July 2022

Produced by Suffolk Archives
The Hold,
131 Fore Street,
Ipswich,
IP4 1LR

www.suffolkarchives.co.uk

All of the stories within this book are based on real Suffolk people and their experiences, as uncovered through Suffolk Archives collections.

The stories have all been written by University of Suffolk MA Creative and Critical Writing Students, and illustrated by BA Graphic Design and Illustration students.

Cover art and illustrations produced by Sammi Wong and Isla Gillett. Book design, typesetting and pagination by Sharna McHardy and Vyara Minkova.

Project supervisors Jane Hackett, Lecturer in Graphic Design and Illustration, Dr Lindsey Scott, Lecturer in English Literature and Emily Shepperson, Suffolk Archives.

FOR ALL THE YOUNG REBELS OF SUFFOLK

FOREWORD
A. M. HOWELL

Do you always like doing as you are told? I certainly didn't when I was young and still don't now! I used to read under the covers with a torch long after I was told to switch off the light, desperate to see what the characters in my book would do next. I chose to wear clumpy boots and ripped jeans instead of pretty dresses that caused my mum and dad to roll their eyes in disapproval. I even went through a horrid phase when I was around three of ripping up the books on my parents' shelves. Apparently, the ripping stopped when I learned how to read, so I like to think this was just me expressing my love for books in an unusual way!

But of course, these were only small acts of rebellion and had few consequences for me, unlike some of the acts undertaken by the real people in this incredible story collection, who are often fighting against the odds.

Many of the child characters you will meet in these stories are fictional, but the rebellious figures they encounter are absolutely real. Take, for example, the story of young Bran, who watched Boudica, queen of the Iceni tribe, as she courageously tore through the streets of Colchester on her chariot, seeking vengeance for her lands being taken by the Romans. Then let's skip forward around two thousand years to the tale of Alice and her heart-warming encounter with Fritz Ball, a cellist who survived huge hardships as a Jewish refugee in Newmarket during the Second World War. Now let's leap back in time again to the year 869AD and meet Bearn, a boy who witnessed

King Edmund's death during a Viking invasion and had a close encounter with a mysterious wolf who guarded the king's severed head. Bury St Edmunds, my adopted hometown, became a place of pilgrimage because of this incident, and you are likely to see statues of King Edmund and the wolf around the town if you ever visit.

The courage, bravery, and rebellious natures of these figures from East Anglia have given me a thirst for delving deeper into the past and finding out more about who these characters were and what they did. You see, I also write historical mysteries for children set in this region, and one thing I always do is make sure the characters in my stories are standing up for what they believe in and are a little rebellious, too. The writers and artists of these stories, all students of creative writing and graphic design at the University of Suffolk, have quite rebellious natures themselves. You will see this on every page, but especially, perhaps, in the words spoken to twelve-year-old Ivy by Nina Layard, a pioneering female archaeologist who moved to Ipswich in the late nineteenth century:

"The most important thing is to be curious, to ask questions and to look for the answers yourself."

I hope these stories might inspire you to do the same.

Happy reading!

A. M. Howell

CONTENTS

PART ONE

ALICE'S BIRTHDAY SURPRISE 10

WHEN LIZZIE MET PHYLLIS 15

THE SERVANT GIRL'S SECRET 19

WORLDS BENEATH THEIR FEET 24

THE PRINCESS GARDEN 29

FINDING VICTOR 33

PART TWO

THE WORLD-RENOWNED LADY PARACHUTIST 40

AN EXTRA AMOUNT OF DARING 46

BOUDICA, ANGEL OF VENGEANCE 50

BEARN AND THE KING'S WOLF 55

THOMAS SAVES THE FISHING FLEET 60

PART THREE

EDWARD AND THE WITCH TRIALS 66

UNE JOURNÉE MISÉRABLE 71

BASIL'S NIGHT WITH THE STARS 75

TO SEE AND TO SPEAK 80

THE PRINCE OF MANY FEATHERS 84

SUFFOLK MAP

THETFORD

The Duleep Singh Sisters

NEWMARKET

Fritz Ball

HINTLESHA

Anges Olive Beam

KESSINGLAND

Victor Barker

IPSWICH

Nina Layard &
Margaret Catchpole

ALICE'S BIRTHDAY SURPRISE
DINAH COWAN

1940, Newmarket

Alice was shooed into the walled garden of Palace House Stables by her foster mother, Edith Harper, who was paying a visit to one of the refugees living there.

"Don't got making a nuisance of yourself, stay out of sight!"

Alice removed her beret and tucked it into her coat pocket. The soft autumn light sparkled through the trees and danced upon the pale stone walls. Normally she enjoyed exploring, but nothing could lift her spirits today.

She was sitting on a bench, chewing her thumbnail, when the man appeared. Alice watched his slow progress across the lawn. He was carrying a cup and saucer in each hand, clearly focused on balancing the contents.

"Good afternoon," he said. "I'm Fritz. And you, I believe, are Alice."

"Yes, how –"

"Ah, Mrs Harper has told me about her young evacuee from London. May I join you?"

Alice accepted the proffered cup, noticing the disfigurement of Fritz's fingers. He took a sip of tea and sighed.

"Now," he said, "I don't mean to pry, but I understand you're a little homesick today?"

Alice blushed and looked down at her fingernails.

"I'll be twelve in a few days," she murmured. "It's the first birthday I won't spend with my family."

She looked up at Fritz, at the kind eyes behind their round spectacles.

"I know rather a lot about homesickness myself," he said.

"You're a refugee?"

Fritz nodded. "I was a lawyer in Germany, until the Nazis banned Jewish people from such professions. Then I was imprisoned, twice, just for being Jewish."

Alice listened as Fritz explained that in one camp, forced labour over a bitter winter gave him frostbite, severely damaging his fingers.

"That was a terrible blow," he said. "You see, I am a cellist. I could no longer hold the bow to play."

"That's awful."

"But I learned to play again, eventually. Months of trying and failing. In that last camp, the hope of playing the cello again kept me going."

Fritz then explained that his own children lived in different parts of the world.

"My eldest boy emigrated to America. My two younger sons are living in Sussex."

"I am so sorry," said Alice, wiping her cheeks.

"We have hope, Alice. Do you write a journal? I find that helps. It's a little like talking to a friend who never interrupts." He winked and she laughed. "But most of all, we have music. It convinces me there is still beauty to be found, even when the world is at its ugliest. Now, how about some Lebkuchen. I believe it's quite similar to your English gingerbread."

*

On the morning of Alice's birthday, Mrs Harper announced that she needed to go back to Palace House Stables.

"Perhaps you could come along, see the horses as a birthday treat?"

When they arrived, Mrs Harper ushered her into the hallway.

"Just wait in there," she said, gesturing to a closed door.

"I won't be a tick."

Alice opened the door and gasped. The drawing room was full of people sitting on rows of chairs.

And there, right at the front, was Fritz, with his cello.

He smiled broadly and nodded at the man seated at the piano and the woman standing beside it.

The music was instantly recognisable, the woman's voice beautiful as she sang Happy Birthday! Alice stood with her hands on her cheeks. She felt a hand on her arm and turned to see Mrs Harper smiling. She let herself be guided to one of the chairs in the front row.

The musicians played on, switched to elaborate, rousing compositions. Alice had never heard anything so magnificent. She was transfixed by Fritz's

performance, and with each dip and glide of the bow, each swell of the music, her heart soared. She let the tears fall, for these were no longer tears of sadness, but of wonder, and hope.

When the final note faded, Alice and the rest of the audience were on their feet. The musicians bowed.

"Ladies and Gentlemen," said Fritz, finally. "My wife, Eva, has made us the largest Marmorkuchen." He smiled at Alice. "Your birthday cake, German style."

The cake was delicious. Alice was just licking the last crumbs from her fork when Fritz approached.

"I don't know how to thank you," she whispered.

Fritz smiled. "It was a pleasure. And this is just a little something for you to open later." He handed her a small package. Alice looked up into those kind eyes and flung her arms around him.

*

That evening, Alice peeled back the paper to reveal a journal, bound in beautiful blue leather. Inside was an inscription.

To Alice,

A place for your happy thoughts, joyful memories. And hope.

From your friend, Fritz Ball.

WHEN LIZZIE MET PHYLLIS
HOLLY TURNER

1977, Hintlesham

One breezy Sunday afternoon, Lizzie went on her own secret adventure in the woods beside her house.

She climbed up and down many trees, swinging on their branches like a chimpanzee. As she climbed higher, she saw her house and her neighbours' houses, all the way down to the end of the street. But one particular house drew Lizzie's gaze. It belonged to Miss Beamish, and her garage door was open.

Inside, Lizzie spotted a huge purple and green flag flapping on the wall. It reminded her of a history lesson she had taken earlier that week.

She scurried down the tree and ran all the way to Miss Beamish's garage.

"Wow, Miss Beamish, your flag!"

"Hello Lizzie." Miss Beamish grinned over her shoulder. "And how many times have I told you to call me Olive?" She laughed and glanced at the flag.

"Where did you get it?"

"A friend of mine called Phyllis Brady gave it to me."

Lizzie walked further into the garage. Beside the flag was a large cream sign saying Votes For Women.

"Was Phyllis one of those who fought for women's rights and the vote?"

Miss Beamish filled a cardboard box with some oddities. "Yes, she was a suffragette. She and I had some rather wild and wonderful adventures together, back then."

Lizzie sat on a wooden chair.

"What was she like?"

Miss Beamish raised an eyebrow.

"She was an interesting woman … always fighting for what was right. But by doing so, she got into a fair bit of trouble."

"How come?" Lizzie was shocked at the thought of someone getting into trouble simply for doing what was right.

"Well," said Miss Beamish, "if I tell you, it must stay a secret between us, okay?"

Lizzie nodded and leaned forwards.

"Phyllis marched in the streets holding signs about women's rights. She also caused chaos by carrying dangerous explosives inside her handbag."

"No way!" Lizzie gasped.

Miss Beamish nodded.

"She did it so that women could have more freedom. But one day, Phyllis got into trouble and went to jail."

"What happened?"

"Her voice was too loud, her beliefs too strong."

"That's crazy."

"What's even crazier is that she never got caught for setting fire to the railway station."

Lizzie gawped at the idea, but then she burst out laughing. Miss Beamish laughed, too.

"That is crazy."

After the laughter died down, Lizzie got up and started looking through the cardboard boxes. There were old photographs of Phyllis marching on the streets and getting arrested as she smiled proudly wearing her purple, green and white brooch and her Votes For Women badge.

"Miss Beamish, why do you have all of Phyllis' things?"

Miss Beamish sighed. "Well, she asked me to look after them while she took a break in the countryside."

Lizzie smiled and continued to peer inside the boxes. She found Phyllis' journal, tucked away beneath some books. She flicked to a page which recorded her time in jail. It was all about how she refused to eat the food.

Lizzie felt a hard lump rise inside her throat. In her history lesson, she had heard all about the hunger strikes of the suffragettes, how they had starved themselves out of protest.

For almost an hour, she asked Miss Beamish more questions about Phyllis. Then she heard her mother calling her in for dinner and she frowned.

"Miss Beamish," she whispered, "I'll come back next week. Then will you tell me more about the rebel Phyllis?"

Miss Beamish chuckled and nodded. Lizzie thanked her and ran off home.

The next day, Lizzie had her history class again. On the tables were some photographs of the different individuals who had fought for women's rights.

Immediately, Lizzie grabbed one particular photograph.

Her eyes lit up with pride as she held on to Phyllis's picture, wishing that Miss Beamish was with her now so that she could see this.

When she flipped the photograph over, on the back, written in pencil, were the words Agnes Olive Beamish.

Lizzie sat there, puzzled. She scrunched up her eyebrows, trying to riddle it out as the teacher approached.

"Lizzie, is everything okay?"

"Yes, Miss Dean. It's just … this photograph. It has my neighbour's name on the back of it, but she told me this was her friend, Miss Phyllis Brady."

Miss Dean looked both bewildered and astonished.

"Well, clearly your neighbour is a rather magnificent woman, Lizzie, with her own secret adventures to tell. She was a strong, independent woman who fought for equality."

In that moment, Lizzie realised that Phyllis Brady, the rebellious suffragette who had done so many wonderful things for women, was actually Miss Beamish, the ordinary woman who lived down the road.

THE SERVANT GIRL'S SECRET
ROSE DAWN

1797, Ipswich

Clara carried the tea tray into the parlour – a dull job for a bright twelve-year-old girl you might say, but Clara loved serving tea, because she got to overhear all the secret discussions between her employer, Mrs Elizabeth Cobbold, and her esteemed visitors.

Today's guest was a finely dressed young woman whose appearance was tarnished by the thick layer of mud caked upon her boots. She spoke confidently to Mrs Cobbold as if they were old friends, but Clara had not seen this woman before today.

She placed the tray upon the table and curtsied.

"Elizabeth, who is this fine young girl you have in your employment? Not trying to replace me, are you?" The mystery guest laughed and winked.

"You'll have to excuse my guest, Clara. This is Miss Margaret Catchpole. She held your position prior to your employment here."

"And a fine servant I was," said Miss Catchpole. "One time, when Mrs Cobbold was sick, I rode for eight miles to find a doctor who was able to nurse her back to health."

'Yes, Margaret," said Mrs Cobbold, "and I can never repay you for that act of kindness. But Clara has many jobs to attend to now."

Mrs Cobbold gestured for Clara to leave, but Miss Catchpole stopped her again.

"Wait! Clara, before you go, take this for your troubles."

She handed her a small square of cake from the tray.

Clara bobbed a small curtsy and hurried out of the room.

But she remained just shy of the doorway, listening.

"Margaret, tell me, you're not still involved with that smuggler, Laud, are you?"

There was a long pause.

"You can't help what the heart wants, Elizabeth. I'm afraid he's stolen my heart and thrown away the key …"

Clara listened intently, scoffing her cake.

A smuggler? And Miss Catchpole in love with him?

She wiped her mouth and hurried to the servants' quarters before she was caught.

*

As Clara lay in bed, she could not forget the words of Miss Catchpole. She couldn't imagine being so strong – to follow her heart and escape the life of a servant girl.

Just then, she heard a loud clatter from outside her bedchambers.

It sounded as if it came from the stables.

Clara crept out of bed, tiptoed past the other sleeping servants, and crouched behind a low wall opposite the stables. She was unable to distinguish the shadows, but she could hear noises coming from inside, as though someone was preparing to ride.

Suddenly, a smartly dressed figure on horseback galloped out of the block. Clara watched open-mouthed as the horse jumped the fence and took off into the distance, disappearing over the horizon.

Upon hearing the commotion, the other servants ran into the yard, yelling in confusion. Clara slipped away, back into her bed. But she knew she wouldn't be able to sleep. Her heart hammered inside her chest.

*

The next day, Clara went to serve tea to her mistress again, but today, Mrs Cobbold sat alone.

She sighed as she read a letter, throwing it down in disgust.

Clara curtsied and turned, but Mrs Cobbold's voice called her back.

"My dear Clara. It seems our unfortunate friend Miss Catchpole has got herself into some trouble." She tapped the letter with a sharp fingernail. "Last night, she stole a horse from our stables. They want to imprison her and put her to death, but I will not let them. She has done wrong, but she is a strong-willed woman who deserves a second chance …"

Clara couldn't believe her ears. The figure she saw was Miss Catchpole! But where was she going? To run away with her smuggler?

"Mrs Cobbold, what can you do to help?"

"I shall write to the Chief Constable immediately and petition for her release. Do not worry, my dear girl. This will not be the last we hear of Margaret Catchpole. I'll make sure of it."

*

Many weeks passed with no news. Clara waited anxiously for word of Margaret's trial. Then, when she had begun to lose all hope, a letter arrived.

"Clara! Forget the tea this morning! I have great news to share!"

Clara ran to her mistress's side.

"Margaret has escaped from prison!"

"Is that good news?" Asked Clara. "But where is she now?"

"We do not know, but I can tell you this. Margaret is strong. She is courageous. She will be able to look after herself now that she has her freedom."

Freedom. Clara turned the word over inside her head. She hoped Margaret's freedom would offer her the chance to start again, and she hoped that one day, she too would have as much heart and courage as the servant girl who stole a horse.

WORLDS BENEATH THEIR FEET
ALI DUDENEY

1906, Ipswich

Ivy wrapped a shawl tightly around her shoulders. Her chilly fingers clutched her dad's dinner. A crust of bread and a lump of cheese wrapped in a cloth.

Her mother's voice boomed across the street from the front door.

"Take your dad's dinner to the dig! Surely you can do that right."

Ivy ran down Foxhall Road, her long skirt swishing her ankles. The clinking of digging shovels against stones and men's voices calling to each other reached her ears, so she followed the sounds. Rounding a corner, she saw the muddy pit lying just ahead. In an effort to spot her dad, she failed to look where she was going. She tripped, stumbled and fell head-first towards the hole.

"Hey! Look out!" A woman's voice called.

Ivy felt her body flying, the enormous pit gaping beneath. A scream rose up in her mouth and then a strong hand grasped her arm, pulling her back from the edge.

Ivy's heart was beating like a hammer. She lay sprawled at a woman's feet, gasping with shock.

"Are you alright?"

Ivy opened her empty hands. The threat of tears formed a lump in her throat.

"Where's Dad's dinner?" She whimpered.

"Oh, was that his dinner?" said the woman. "There now, don't cry." In spite of her long skirts, she jumped down onto a plank, shouting to one of the labourers. "Can you reach that for me, please?" She pointed to the small bundle of cloth, still intact.

The package arrived safely into the woman's hands. Ivy took it from her gratefully.

"Thank you."

"Alright now?" she asked, picking up her notebook, pen, and a piece of stone.

Ivy had never seen a woman working in a dig before. She loitered for a few moments, watching and admiring the careful sifting of soil and the retrieval of stones before leaving to find her dad.

*

At home that evening, Ivy asked her dad about the dig.

"What do the ladies do there?"

"They're in charge, they're the archaeologists. They understand the things we dig up, like the stone-age hand axes."

Ivy yearned to know more. Now that she was twelve, she needed to find some work to help support the family.

"Do you think I could ask them for a job, Dad?"

"Whatever next!" Her mother tutted.

"Let her try," her dad told his wife. "If she earns, what does it matter what she does?"

*

Ivy went to the dig with her father the next morning. Miss Nina Layard, the kind woman who had offered her assistance, agreed that Ivy could have a trial week.

"But she must work hard. She'll be treated like everyone else here."

Ivy catalogued pre-historic items with her neat writing, while Miss Mary Outram, Nina's friend, told her what to write. Sometimes special stones were missed, so Ivy had to search through piles of earth, checking to see if anything of value had been overlooked.

"Miss Layard is very clever and knows a lot about the stone-age settlement that was here under our feet," said Miss Outram.

"Are you close friends?" Ivy knew the question was personal, but somehow, she sensed that Miss Outram wouldn't mind.

"As close as can be," Miss Outram replied with a smile.

That afternoon, Miss Layard told Ivy more about the dig.

"Almost a million years ago, people lived here. They didn't have pots and pans and knives like us, so they had to use natural things, like stones shaped in special ways to help them cut meat, for instance." She handed Ivy another sharpened stone.

"It feels alive with the history of a different time," Ivy whispered. The stone's warmth seemed to radiate in her hand.

Later that week, Miss Layard and Miss Outram invited Ivy to tea at their home and showed her some books on archaeology.

"You can borrow this one, if you like," Miss Layard said, handing Ivy a book about the stone age.

"I want to be an archaeologist when I grow up, but I haven't done enough schooling."

"Don't worry about that, Ivy," said Miss Layard with a smile. "Most of what I know I taught myself or learned while travelling. The most important thing is to be curious, to ask questions, and to look for the answers yourself."

After her trial week, Ivy continued to work with Nina and Mary as an assistant. Then one day, on another dig, there was great excitement around the site.

"I've been invited to become a Fellow of the Society of Antiquaries of London!" Nina cried.

"Can women do that?" Ivy asked.

"They can now!" said Mary, grinning and hugging Nina.

THE PRINCESS GARDEN
MOLLY BRITTON

1965, Thetford

"Who lives there?" Lily asked her father, looking up at the light brown brick house.

"Wouldn't you like to know," her father replied, setting down his tools. He had been a groundskeeper at Elveden Hall since before any of his children could remember and coming to work with him was always a special treat.

"So why don't you tell us?" Olivia asked. She was the youngest and had the least understanding of buildings.

"Buildings can stand for centuries, but the families who live in them come and go," he replied, arranging the young flowers that needed to be planted. "Although, there was one family, a very special family, who lived here once upon a time."

"Who were they?" asked Abi, the middle child. Her full name was Abigail, but she much preferred Abi, and her face was lit up with interest.

"The Duleep Singhs. Grab a trowel from over there and I'll tell you all about them while we work."

The girls knelt down beside their father and started to dig.

"Once upon a time," he murmured, "long, long ago, there lived three princesses with no kingdom, much like the lot of you. Their father, Sir Duleep

Singh, had his kingdom taken from him by The British Empire, headed up by Queen Victoria, and in return, had been sent to Britain. The oldest of the princesses was Bamba Duleep Singh. Then came her sister, Catherine. Finally, there was Sophia, the youngest. They lived in that house, Elveden Hall, safely with their father."

"Where was their mum?" Olivia asked.

Their father's eyes glazed over and he cleared his throat before he spoke.

"She, er … she died. When the youngest daughter was very young."

"Like mummy?" Olivia asked.

Their father nodded, and for a moment, the spell of his beguiling tale was broken. He returned his attention to the plants beside him, and the soft holes in the earth that his daughters were digging. Finally, the magic in his voice returned.

"Bamba, as the oldest, grew up and took care of her family. She didn't stop there, though. She travelled the world. She stayed for years in India, which is where her family were from, to help more people. And while she was there, she fought for Indian independence from Great Britain. In her old age, she returned to England and worked to preserve the legacy of her family."

The girls nodded, tucking away loose hairs and rolling up their sleeves with muddied fingers as they listened.

"Catherine travelled the world, too. She travelled very far, until she and her friend, Lina, settled in Germany. Catherine also helped people. She held them to get out of Germany when it stopped being safe for them to be there, back at the start of World War Two."

The girls dug deeper, but tenderly, scooping out the soil and pushing it to one side as they worked.

"And Sophia, the youngest, was a suffragette. She fought for the rights of women alongside other suffragettes, like Emmeline Pankhurst. When World War One began, Sophia became a nurse, helping soldiers who were injured in the war."

The girls stopped and looked at their father, wide-eyed at the story of the princesses. He bit his cheek to keep from laughing at their matching grins.

"And what's best about it," he finished, "is that they all started here, just like the three of you." He placed the flowers into the holes and guided his daughters in scooping the dirt and compost over them.

"Lily, will you get the watering can?"

Lily clambered to her feet, clapping her hands to shake off the muck, and grabbed the heavy can.

"You know the deal, Lil," her father reminded her, "one third each.'

Lily nodded, pouring one third of the can over the newly planted flowers. "I think Bamba is my favourite," she said thoughtfully, "she took care of her family when they needed her."

Lily passed the can to Abi, and Abi took her turn pouring. "I like Catherine," she said, "she helped people who were in danger."

Olivia took the can for her third. "Sophia was the best. She helped everyone, and she was in the war. She's the best."

"No, Bamba's the best because she's the oldest." Lily said haughtily.

"No, Catherine's the best, she fought Nazis!" Abi cried, jumping to her feet.

"Sophia's great, too!' Olivia shouted, waving her arms.

The groundskeeper watched his children bicker from where he knelt on the ground. Then he cast his eyes up to the heavens and smiled.

With debating skills like this, their daughters would do great things, too.

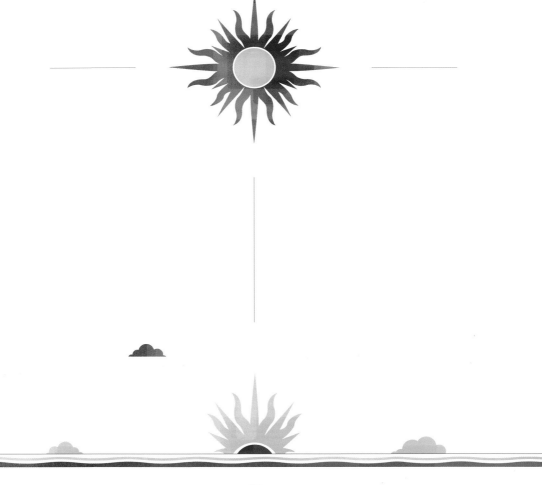

FINDING VICTOR
AMBER SPALDING

Present Day, Suffolk

Isobel woke to cold and bare legs. Her mother had pulled off the duvet, leaving her exposed to the chilly winter morning.

"Isobel! You'd better be moving up there!"

Isobel rolled over and was struck by the time on the clock.

7:53 am.

She was late.

After running in the frosty air, the school corridors felt hot and stuffy. The other children ignored her, nudging her as they walked past.

"Look," one girl whispered, loud enough so Isobel could hear, "she looks just like a boy."

"I know!" said the other girl. "No one's ever going to love her like that …"

Isobel pulled at her shirt.

"Miss Isobel," called a stern voice from behind, "are you coming to class this morning, or are we just going to stand there gawping?"

"Sorry, Miss Herald."

Isobel scurried into the classroom and sat in the only space available – at the front.

"So, class," exclaimed Miss Herald, "today we are learning about individuals who have gone above and beyond to challenge the way we think."

Isobel tried to listen as Mrs Herald rattled through names from history – war heroes, convicts, queens – but she was distracted by the two girls still whispering behind. She wanted to go back under the bed covers where she could be alone.

Just as she was about to lose herself to these thoughts, Miss Herald's voice boomed across the room.

"Colonel Victor Barker, born in 1895, led an extraordinary life."

Isobel thought it was going to be another name and story she didn't understand, but as Miss Herald continued, she began to feel differently.

"Assigned female at birth, Barker grew up as a woman, married, and joined the Women's Auxiliary Air Force. But after the marriage fell apart in 1923, Barker assumed the identity of a man and fell in love with a woman."

Isobel gulped. All she could think about was Barker's disguise. She thought about their clothes, their military uniform, their suits, how they had fooled everyone. How they must have felt free.

"Barker was arrested in 1929 on the account of perjury. While at Brixton Prison, their assigned sex of female was revealed, and they were transferred to Holloway Prison for Women."

Isobel stared out of the window. She knew it was wrong to compare, but sometimes, school felt like her own prison.

That evening, she tucked herself away inside her bedroom and started investigating like a detective, unpicking Barker's life bit by bit until she understood their journey. Even when her mother called her down for dinner, she refused.

"I'll eat later!"

Isobel grew so fascinated by Barker's experiences that she couldn't stop digging. She felt like a pirate, searching for buried treasure. Reflecting on their identity made her reflect on her own. Her whole life, she'd been dressing to please others, and when she did try to embrace herself, she was bullied for it. Her mother told her it was okay, but that wasn't enough. So Isobel read until the early hours and feel asleep surrounded by papers, the details of Barker's life spread over her like a blanket.

*

Isobel's alarm rang early next morning. She hit snooze and rolled over, but as she closed her eyes, a voice inside her head started grumbling.

Pssst, Isobel. Wake up!

Isobel sat up, confused.

"Am I going mad?" she asked.

No. It's me. Colonel Barker …

"Wait a minute – how are you –"

Listen! We don't have much time!

Isobel did as the voice asked and listened.

I spent most of my childhood unsure of myself. I don't want you to feel like that.

"But I don't know how to be myself."

Yes, you do. It's right here, inside of you.

Isobel shook her head.

It doesn't matter what you wear. What matters is that you feel comfortable.

"How can I be comfortable when no one is comfortable with me?"

Because I believe in you, said Colonel Barker, and if you believe in yourself, others will follow.

"Isobel!" her mother called. "Are you awake yet?"

Isobel blinked. The room was empty.

"Yes, Mum, I'm just getting dressed."

But Isobel didn't get dressed. At least, not yet.

Instead, she stretched herself, returned to her notes and finished her school project.

*

With the story complete, Isobel finally found the courage to be herself. She rummaged inside her drawers and found a pair of black school trousers and a baseball cap. They slipped on like a glove. Isobel grinned.

She marched into the kitchen with Barker's story tucked firmly under her arm.

"Mum, look." She put her hands in her pockets. "I've done it. I'm never going back."

Her mother smiled.

"And who do I have the pleasure of meeting?"

"Victor," he said. "You can call me Victor."

SUFFOLK MAP

BURY ST EDMUNDS

Saint Edmund

COLCHESTER

Boudica

LOWESTOFT

Thomas Crisp

ALDEBURGH

Elizabeth Garrett Anderson

PSWICH

ith Maud Cook

THE WORLD-RENOWNED LADY PARACHUTIST

CAROLINE ROBERTS

1909, East Anglia

Martha stood still, gazing around at the attractions. It was finally her twelfth birthday and they had come to an air show.

The field was scattered with people. Men in straw hats and ladies in headscarves moved between the small planes and huge baskets. One or two balloons towered above them, waving gently in the still summer air. The day was perfect, with the kind of blue skies and wispy, candyfloss clouds that make you sigh and wish you could lay in a field staring at them all day.

As her brothers wrestled with one another on the grass, Martha wondered how it would be to soar through the air. For as long as she could remember, she had wanted to fly.

Martha's dad squeezed her hand.

"What are you most excited about seeing?"

"Viola, of course," said Martha. "The Lady Parachutist!"

A star attraction at the show was a parachute jump, and a daring performer called Viola Spencer was billed to appear. Martha daydreamed about what this marvel of the skies might look like. Would she be tall and strong? Or have enormous wings on her back?

Martha's brothers nudged each other.

"It's a man in disguise!"

"Girls can't fly!"

Martha ignored them and helped her mum unpack the lunch. There were huge chunks of freshly baked bread, a pat of butter as golden as a daffodil, a square of crumbly cheese wrapped in wax paper, and a fruit cake bulging with sultanas and plump round cherries.

Suddenly, a ripple of noise made Martha turn. She scrambled up, dropping her cake on the blanket and running towards a crowd gathered on the other side of the field.

"Not too close!" shouted her mum.

As Martha reached them, an "Ooohh" rang out and a small balloon pulled up into the air. Beneath it, holding onto a circus-like trapeze, was a figure dressed in red-laced boots, matching trousers and a long, smart jacket, belted at the waist.

Viola.

Craning her neck, Martha held her breath as the balloon went up and up. Then she blinked.

Something seemed wrong.

The balloon had started to deflate.

Martha gasped, putting her hand to her mouth as the figure fell. The parachute opened and Viola was propelled into the air before drifting towards the next field, blown off course by a gust of warm air.

Martha ran. She had to be the first to see if Viola was alright.

The woman landed on the ground and rolled over and over, the parachute whoomphing down on top of her and wrapping her up.

"Are you alright?" Martha panted.

"Absolutely," said Viola, jumping up to brush herself off and grinning. "Phew, that was a good one!"

Martha grinned, too. Then she looked down at the mess.

"Give me a hand?" asked Viola.

Martha helped Viola to gather up the parachute, taming its huge billowing folds of red fabric until the last section was caught up in Viola's arms. Together, they walked back to the air show.

"What does it feel like, being up there?"

Viola smiled.

"Like being free."

"Aren't you scared?" Martha's heart beat in her chest as she imagined herself jumping through the air.

"A little," Viola confided. "But it's also exhilarating. Do you know, I ran away from home to go on my first balloon flight? I suppose I was only a little older than you are now!"

"Goodness," said Martha, trying to imagine her brothers' reactions if she ran away with Viola right now.

"I've been training ever since then, and in December, I'm going to France to learn how to fly a plane."

"Really?" Martha gasped. "Can women do that?"

Viola lifted her gaze and looked straight ahead.

"Well, I'm sure some would say they couldn't, but I'm going to do it anyway. And one day, I'm going to fly across the channel."

Martha's breath caught in her throat.

"I think that's incredible," she whispered.

They reached the field and Viola stopped, holding out her hand for Martha to shake it.

"Nice to meet you! I forgot to ask your name."

"It's Martha."

"Well, thanks for your help, Martha." Then she whispered, "and my real name is Edith Cook."

Edith strode off into the excited crowd, leaving Martha staring after her.

Martha re-joined her family on the blanket, eager to tell them all about Viola. A small plane buzzed overhead and she lifted her hand to shield her eyes, squinting against the sun.

Martha thought of Edith and imagined her flying it. Brave and daring as always, grinning, and holding the plane steady.

As it soared higher into the air, Martha smiled, knowing that if Edith could do it, so could she.

"One day," she whispered to herself. "One day."

AN EXTRA AMOUNT OF DARING
EMILY GENTRY

1872, Queen Elizabeth Hospital for Children, London

Beth watched the hospital staff with a glum expression. It had been ages since the doctor had said he would come and talk to her about her operation. She drew up her knees and hugged them. The operation would make her feel better (at least, that's what her mother said) but all she wanted was to be back at home in her own bed, under soft, clean sheets.

Trying to ignore the nerves in her stomach and the itchiness of the rough, worn blanket, she turned her attention to the comings and goings of the ward. Several people, including the doctor who had promised to come and talk to her, were gathered around the main desk. There were three nurses there in puffy-sleeved white uniforms, and another woman, wearing a dove-grey dress with a crisp white coat over the top. Beth would have thought she was a doctor, if she hadn't known such a thing to be impossible. Women simply couldn't do such things.

After a few moments, the woman looked up at her and smiled. Then she excused herself and came over.

"Hello there. It's Beth, isn't it?"

Lost for words, Beth could only nod.

"You're having your appendix out, I believe." The woman smiled again. "You look a little nervous – I'm guessing this is your first time staying in a hospital?"

When Beth remained quiet, the woman sat on the edge of her bed and sighed.

"I'm sorry, I've been incredibly rude. I know your name, but you don't know mine." She held out her hand. "I'm Elizabeth Garrett Anderson, but you may call me Elizabeth. I'm one of the doctors looking after you."

Beth's head shot up. So she really was a doctor!

Solemnly, she shook Elizabeth's hand. Before she could say anything, quick footsteps marched towards them.

"Don't you have other things to be doing, Elizabeth?"

The male doctor paused at the foot of the bed, looking down at them.

"Hello, Dr Smith. I was planning to check on my other patients once I'd finished talking with Beth here." Elizabeth straightened her shoulders. "And it's Dr Garrett Anderson, if you don't mind."

Beth watched the exchange with interest. She had never seen a woman stand up for herself in such a way before. Dr Smith lowered his gaze.

"Well, why don't you leave this patient to me? The procedure is complicated, and I'm sure I am more qualified."

Beth found herself intensely disliking Dr Smith.

"Well," said Elizabeth "considering I graduated with the highest marks of our class, I would say I am more than qualified to help Beth." Her voice was composed, but Beth knew something icy lay beneath the surface.

Dr Smith stared at her for a moment. Then he sniffed the air and stalked away down the corridor. Elizabeth watched him disappear through the double doors.

"I'm sorry about that," she said. "Now, where were we?"

Beth stared at her in amazement.

"Were you really?" she managed to say.

"Really what?"

"The one who graduated with the highest marks?"

Elizabeth smiled.

"Yes, I was. I was also the only woman, so you can imagine how my classmates reacted."

Beth giggled. The sound surprised her and she tried to remember the last time she had laughed.

"I didn't think women could become doctors," she said softly. "My father says reading makes them too hysterical and they shouldn't be allowed to study medicine."

Elizabeth laughed. "There were many men who told me something similar when I began studying. They even tried to ban me from attending my lessons!"

Beth thought about this for a moment.

"Could I become a doctor?"

"Of course, you could! That is, it might not be easy, but never let anybody stop you from doing what you want to do."

Beth nodded.

Elizabeth glanced at the watch pinned to her coat.

"It's time for me to go and get ready, but try not to be nervous. It will all be over before you know it."

She went to stand but Beth reached for her arm.

"Will you be doing the operation?"

Elizabeth glanced to where Dr Smith had resurfaced with one of his male colleagues.

"No, I'll be assisting. But don't worry. Dr Smith may come off as rude, but he's actually very good at his job."

She stood up and smoothed down the skirts of her dress.

"How are you feeling now?'

Beth considered this, then smiled.

"Much better, thank you."

"Good. Then I'll see you after the operation."

Beth watched Elizabeth go, excitement fluttering inside her chest. She ran her fingers over the bed's worn blanket. Perhaps it didn't feel so rough, after all.

BOUDICA, ANGEL OF VENGEANCE
JORDAN GELLER

AD 60-61, Camulodunum (Colchester)

Bran of the Iceni tribe had only seen twelve summers when the revolt happened. His lanky, nimble frame gave him the uncanny ability to slink into the darkness, with only his bright red hair lighting him up in the undergrowth. His talent at hiding impressed his queen, Boudica, so she made him a scout for her army – to run ahead of his marching kinsmen, spy on the Roman invaders and report what he had seen.

For several days, Bran watched from a tree over the settlement of Camulodunum, perched like a curious raven.

"From here, I will see everything," he whispered to the birds around him.

Most of the Roman soldiers had left for parts unknown, filing out of the stony walls like a trail of ants.

And Bran knew. Now was the time for his queen to strike.

He gave the signal to another scout in a distant tree, who faded away into the undergrowth like a ghost. The boy would not join the fight itself—Boudica forbade that, for she valued his scouting skills too much. But Bran wanted nothing more than to fight for his queen – a woman wronged by the invaders. He remembered her marriage to King Prasutagus, who struck a deal with the Romans to ensure his kingdom passed to Boudica on the event of his death. But when Prasutagus died, the Romans were quick to swoop in and break their empty promises.

Bran gritted his teeth as he remembered the Romans sneering as they cracked the whip at Boudica and her daughters. They wanted to take everything, not just from Boudica, but from the entire Iceni Tribe.

"My tribe," Bran murmured.

Boudica called the Iceni men to her side and made her own promises that would never be broken.

"Nothing is safe from Roman pride and arrogance. Win the battle or perish, that is what I will do as a woman!"

And so, the sacking of Camulodunum began.

The Romans never knew what was coming. They were too comfortable in their bath houses and temples when the fires of the Iceni washed over them. The fire of rebellion had come for the invaders at long last. Bran watched on as his fellow Celts broke down the gates to the city and were met with fresh-faced Roman guards caught unaware of the attack. Their spears and shields were no match for the Iceni, who would not live under thumb and heel of the Roman Empire.

Bran felt he had to get closer, so he hopped from his tree and scaled the city walls. In the chaos, he snuck through the fighting warriors, unnoticed by all. He crouched atop a battlement, observing everything, and that was when his eyes lit up with worry.

Out of nowhere, a unit of Romans rushed at the Iceni and drove them back. They laid their shields in front and on top, creating a tortoise formation. The Iceni arrows bounced off the walking tortoise shell, which now snaked around the narrow streets like a centipede.

"I cannot sit here and watch my tribe get hurt!"

But for the first time, Bran felt hopeless.

That feeling lasted, until he heard the clattering of horse hooves on stone cobbles.

Bran looked down and saw a mane of fire billowing in the wind. Flames erupted all around the city, heralding the arrival of the almighty Iceni queen. Bran abandoned his cover and cheered as her horse-drawn chariot stampeded through the Roman line. Boudica held her arms up, a spear in one hand, and said nothing, for nothing needed to be said – the look of shock and fear upon the enemy faces said it all.

The Iceni rallied and roared for their queen, following in her wake. With the flames all-consuming, Bran's eyes began to lose focus, but he knew what he saw. Boudica, the avenging angel, had come, riding atop a chariot of fire, its wheels burning through the falling darkness. There was a fire in her belly that burned fiercer than her red hair. She was the fire of the Iceni tribe that would never burn out. Within seconds, Boudica's chariot ripped through the Roman tortoise and scattered its pieces to the wind. The invaders retreated as Boudica tore through the streets of Camulodunum, inspiring her people to continue the fight.

And fight they did, until the city fell within the night.

Over the years, Bran stayed at his queen's side. Next, he would scout out the Roman capital of Londinium, another victory to add to her growing legend. Eventually, Boudica would fall against the mounting Roman legions, but she did so without fear or regret. Bran would never forget her, and he knew that history would remember the almighty Iceni queen.

BEARN AND THE KING'S WOLF
JAMES BROWN

AD 869, East Anglia

Bearn swung a wooden sword around his head and stabbed at the Great Oak tree that stood beside him and his father. As the two great armies battled below their position on the large hill that overlooked the field, Bearn spotted his hero, King Edmund. He twirled on his heels and delivered another blow to the tree.

"A great victory for Bearn and his brave King Edmund!"

"Yes, Son," said Cuthred, lifting his walking stick and slicing it through the air as if it too were a sword. "Our King is certainly the bravest."

But as the battle raged on, Bearn's heart sank. The invading Vikings surrounded the outer battlefield and launched many arrows towards Edmund and his soldiers. The Viking shouts of triumph grey louder as Edmund's army became quieter and fell back. Eventually, Cuthred grabbed his son's arm.

"Quickly, now, Bearn, we must go."

"No, Father. I want to stay."

"All is lost, my boy. The King has been captured."

Before Bearn could see it for himself, Cuthred led him away to their horse. Bearn helped his father into the saddle, then they rode back towards the village with haste.

*

In the next few days, word reached the villagers that King Edmund had been killed. Cuthred took his son rabbit hunting so they could be distracted from the terrible news.

"The king never relented. He would not renounce his faith, even when facing death." Cuthred clenched his teeth. He seemed to be speaking more to himself than his son as they walked through the great forest.

"Well, what did they expect?" said Bearn, fighting back the tears. "My King was born on the day of Yule."

"More than that, Son," said Cuthred, his face filled with pride. "No number of arrows fired towards him would change his mind."

Bearn's father paused for a moment.

"Our people found him on a tree," he whispered. "I'm afraid they took his head."

Bearn turned from his father as he felt tears sting his eyes. He walked toward a large tree, pulled out his wooden sword and threw it at the trunk, a howl of rage coming from deep within him.

Just then, a monstrous grey wolf emerged from the bushes.

It stood in front of Bearn, howling.

"Dad …" the boy cried. "There's a wolf …"

Thick slobber dripped from its large, sharp teeth.

The wolf howled again, and Bearn's blood ran cold. He reached down, smoothly pulled the wooden sword up out of the leaves. Holding it in front of him, he spoke loud and clear.

"In the name of King Edmund, I command you to leave."

The wolf snarled. Its lips pulled back from its teeth, revealing a terrifying grin.

Bearn stood his ground, rooted to the spot as Cuthred appeared.

"Stay where you are, Bearn ..."

His father touched the handle of his own steel sword.

Several moments passed before anything moved. Then finally, the wolf lowered its head. Slowly, it turned and stalked through the bushes, back in the direction it had come from.

*

The next day, Bearn and his father walked through the village. They heard a call and Bearn turned. It was his uncle, running towards them, puffing and panting.

"Have you heard?" asked Uncle Eldred. "There's been a miracle."

Bearn looked up at his father.

"Well, what is it, Eldred?" Cuthred sounded impatient.

"A wolf," he murmured. "It howled to the men searching for the King's head. And when they eventually found the wolf, it was guarding the head, like a dog sitting beside its master."

Bearn shivered. He felt certain that the wolf from the woods was the very same beast that had kept watch over his King.

"And that's not all," said Eldred, almost shouting in excitement. "When the head and the body were brought together, they reunited as if never separated!"

Whispers and excitement rippled through the village. The news spread through other villages, the towns, and eventually, through the whole of East Anglia.

Bearn wondered what had become of the wolf that had guarded the King's head so loyally. In the months that followed, he dreamed of their encounter in the woods many times, but he never saw it again.

Soon, he began dualling with the air once more as battles continued to rage throughout the land. He eventually became a great warrior himself and would tell the story of King Edmund and the legend of the wolf to his children. And before Bearn's time was over, he was proud to see his King become Saint Edmund, the first patron saint of England.

THOMAS SAVES THE FISHING FLEET
JEREMY EVANS

1917, Lowestoft

William and Elsie stood on the dock of the waterfront sheltering from the cold breeze. They could see the fishing boats coming and going and men hunched over repairing the nets. Other figures stowed crates that would carry the catch. William watched them while his younger sister gazed at the tall, varnished masts under cloudy skies.

Their grandfather came to find them.

"There you are," he panted, taking Elsie's hand. "Now don't get in the way. Fishing smacks are busy boats and these are full of fish. Barely floating they're so full!"

"What's that?" asked William, pulling at his tweed cap. He pointed at the closest of the fishing boats. It had tan sails coiled around the mast and a black hull that looked as if it had been painted a thousand times. But William was interested in something hidden under a blue tarpaulin on the foredeck.

Grandad leaned closer.

"That," he said sternly, "is a ship's gun." He put a finger to his lips. "Loose talk costs lives."

A burly fisherman walked past with a rolling gait as if he were already at sea. Something about him made you watch him. Like he had an inner power.

Ellie twirled in her dress and bonnet.

"Who's he?" she asked.

The man must have heard her. He turned, grinned in a friendly way and winked before going back to his work. As he went to the stern of the ship, they saw its name. The Nelson.

"That's Captain Thomas Crisp," said Grandad.

"Ooh, is he a pirate?"

"Far from it, my girl!" On stiff knees, Grandad crouched beside them. "Thomas Crisp is a war hero."

"Gosh," said William. "But he looks just like a normal fisherman."

"That he does. You see, when the fishing fleet goes out, Thomas Crisp is also going fishing. But on board his fishing boat, under that blue tarpaulin, he has a gun to protect our fish from German U-boats."

"From submarines?" said Elsie.

"That's right," said Grandad. "U-boat submarines. And they sink our fishing boats in the hope that we'll all starve!"

William rubbed his belly, already feeling hungry.

"But we won't!" laughed Grandad, watching him. "Because Thomas Crisp destroyed two submarines only the other day. He saved the fleet."

William felt a glow of pride. The Great War had been very hard on everyone, and having a true hero, right here in Lowestoft, was exciting.

As the ship sailed out of the dock, William and Elsie waved goodbye to Thomas Crisp. William could see the fishing crew and a gunner on board. One of the fishermen looked a lot like Thomas, but younger. William guessed this might be Thomas's son. As the tan sails filled with cold air, the Nelson set out to sea.

"We'll come back tomorrow and see them again," said Grandad.

*

But the next day, the newspapers were filled with another story. The German U-boats had discovered the armed fishing smacks and had targeted the Nelson with their guns.

Thomas Crisp had been shot.

He had died in the arms of his son.

The rest of the crew were rescued but the Nelson had sunk.

"This is terrible," said Elsie. "Thomas has died."

William's eyes filled with tears. "The papers say the U-boats had much bigger guns and the Nelson was over-powered ..." He wiped his cheek furiously. "It's not fair. They couldn't get close enough to shoot back."

After a solemn breakfast, Grandad took them out to the break water. They could see the fleet fishing in the distance.

"See them boats," he said. "They're still fishing because of Thomas Crisp."

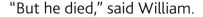

"But he died," said William.

"Yes …" There was a strange look in Grandad's eye.

"You mean he knew?"

"He knew he couldn't win forever."

"So … he gave his life," said Elsie, gazing at the distant ships on the grey North Sea.

"That's right," said Grandad. "The British Prime Minister even stood up and praised our Thomas for his actions in the British Parliament. Everybody admires his courage and commitment to protect us."

Sunlight broke through the clouds. It picked out the swaying waters around the fishing smacks. William stared out at the sea, thinking of the sacrifice one man had made for the good of everybody else. Grandad was right. It was something very courageous indeed.

He vowed to remember what Thomas Crisp had done for Lowestoft and for the country at war. Then he joined his sister and waved to the fishermen working tirelessly to bring in the catch, even though the men were specks on the horizon who could not see their waving hands.

SUFFOLK MAP

RICKINGHALL
Basil Brown

NEWMARKET
Prince Monolulu

WESTHORPE
Mary Tudor

LOWESTOFT

Amy Denny

IPSWICH

Albert Grant

N

W   E

S

EDWARD AND THE WITCH TRIALS
SARAH CLARK

1663, Lowestoft

Edward was on his way home from the market one October afternoon, carrying the juicy red apples he had just bought for his mother, when he bumped into an angry woman standing by the fish sellers.

She was arguing with Samuel Pacy, the fish man.

"Why won't you sell me your fish? I'm as good as anyone living in this town and my family needs to eat!" Her cheeks were bright red as she jabbed her finger at him.

Mr Pacy shook his fist, leaning right up to the woman's face.

"Away with you, Amy Denny," he growled. "My fish is too good for the likes of you and your family. Go on, now, shoo!"

And with that, he waved her off.

Amy Denny stormed away, muttering to herself. Unfortunately, Edward walked straight into her. Apples flew in every direction and his face flushed as he stood there, waiting to be told off.

"I'm s-s-sorry," he stuttered, watching in horror as the apples rolled away down the road.

Amy Denny ran after them. She caught the two apples that had escaped as Edward was picking up another and handed them back to him.

"Never mind, lad," she said kindly. "It was as much my fault as it was yours. I should've been looking where I was going."

She handed him the last apple.

"Food is too precious to lose, is it not?"

Edward nodded. Then he pushed the last apple back into her hand.

Amy Denny smiled.

Edward thanked her, then he ran home as fast as he could, hoping that the apples weren't too bruised. If they were, his mother would surely box his ears.

The next day, Edward saw something very curious. Mr Pacy's daughter, Deborah, rolling around on the ground outside their school, groaning and crying.

She threw back her head, rolled her eyes and shrieked. "That Amy Denny! My father says she's a witch! She's bewitched me!"

Deborah was making horrible noises as if she was going to be sick. Edward left her to her performance. He didn't much like Deborah Pacy. She always teased him, and it suited him to walk away. But why would Mr Pacy say that Amy Denny was a witch?

*

Edward didn't think any more about the strange events of that week, until one day in March, his father was summoned to Bury St Edmunds to talk about what had happened to Deborah Pacy, and her sister, Elizabeth.

Edward had told his father about Deborah's odd behaviour that day. When he asked his father why he was going to the trial, he said, "Mr Pacy says he won't sell us any more fish if I don't tell the judges what you saw. He knows you were there, Edward, and Amy Denny's family are considered troublemakers, anyway."

"But what did she do?" asked Edward.

"They say she's a witch," said his mother, joining them at the kitchen table, "and once you've been accused of that, there's not much you can do.'

"But what if she isn't a witch?" Edward cried. "What if Elizabeth and Deborah Pacy are making everything up?"

"Mr Pacy says the girls have been very sick, Edward."

Edward's mother and father looked at each other then, in a way they often did when they didn't believe Edward had washed his hands before dinner. Something was very wrong.

"Can I come with you?" he asked.

Edward's mother shook her head, but his father touched her gently on the shoulder.

"Margaret, the boy is growing up. He needs to know about these things."

So Edward went along to Bury St Edmunds. He was told to stay very quiet and not interrupt. Even if he really wanted to.

At the hearing, Edward was upset by what he heard. He behaved himself and tried not to say anything, even when the people cried awful things about Amy Denny. And when the men decided that she was definitely a witch, he had to bite his tongue very hard so that he didn't cry out when the sentence of hanging was ordered.

He was the angriest he had ever been, and when he saw the crowd jeering and shouting as Amy Denny and another frightened woman accused of witchcraft were hoisted into the air, he decided that when he was older, something must be done. He would do all he could to help those people who were unable to help themselves.

As Edward walked away, holding the slightly bruised apple his mother had given him that morning, he vowed that he would do this for Amy Denny. And he would never forget the kindness she had shown him, that fateful October afternoon.

UNE JOURNÉE MISÉRABLE
CLAIRE HOLLAND

1508, Richmond Palace

Mary stood alone in the vast empty school room. She'd been taught only French lessons for the past three weeks and couldn't understand why it was suddenly so important.

She was practising her conversation etiquette when at court – "Bonjour, Monsieur, comment allez-vous?" – when one of her attendants entered the room.

"Princess Mary, it's time for your dress fitting."

Mary followed eagerly. She loved the beautiful clothes she got to wear as an English princess. Dresses made from silks, satins, and brocade fabrics with intricately patterned embroidery. Learning to embroider herself, she could understand the hours of arduous work required. But these dresses were also impractical, especially when trying to dance gracefully.

"Oh, how I would love to dance!" said Mary. She did not often get the chance to, unless important visitors came to see father.

As she was having her dress altered, her grandmother, Margaret, came into the room.

"Mary! Do stand still! Rose cannot make the correct alterations unless you stop fidgeting."

"I'm sorry," said Mary, stifling a yawn. "This dress is so heavy and I'm tired."

"Why are you tired?" asked her grandmother.

"I've been spending all my time practising French and Latin. I haven't been allowed to practise my instruments, either."

Mary's grandmother took her by the hand.

"Mary, has no one spoken to you about the important visitors we are having tomorrow and why they are coming?"

Mary shook her head. Her grandmother instructed Rose to leave. Something was very wrong.

"Mary, you are beginning to understand your place in the royal court. You are lucky to have received an education in French and Latin alongside your many other accomplishments. The lessons are to ensure you know how to behave as an English princess. You are thirteen and becoming a woman." Her grandmother cleared her throat. "Your father has decided you are to be married to Prince Charles of Castile. The marriage will take place tomorrow."

Mary opened her mouth to protest but her grandmother shook her head.

"This decision does not belong to you. It belongs to your father, the king, and his decision is final."

Mary only half listened as her grandmother explained that it was to be a proxy marriage – a wedding in which one or both individuals are not present. Charles, her future husband, would not be attending. He was only eight years old. A representative had been sent on his behalf.

The conversation was over. Rose was called back into the room to complete the alterations and Mary was instructed to practise her French again before she went to bed. She would need to speak in French at the ceremony the following day.

*

Mary went to bed that night with questions whirling around her head. When would she meet Charles? Why was she being made to marry an eight-year-old boy she had never met? And would she be sent away to live with him?

She understood now why she had been allowed to give out prizes at jousts during recent events and why she had been permitted to have chaperoned dances.

She thought about her brother Henry, Prince of Wales, and how one day, he would be king. Although they lived in separate households, they were close. Would this change anything? And if she spoke to him, could she persuade him to let her marry someone she knew and loved?

*

The next day, Mary awoke on the morning of her wedding, hoping that the conversation with her grandmother was just a miserable dream.

But it was no dream.

Soon she was being attended by servants helping her to prepare for the ceremony. The dress now fit perfectly, but it had never felt heavier.

The Archbishop of Canterbury conducted parts of the ceremony in Latin, and although Mary had received lessons in Latin, she struggled to follow what was being said. Her brother, Henry, was among the many people watching.

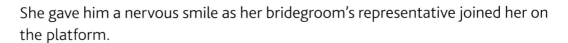

She gave him a nervous smile as her bridegroom's representative joined her on the platform.

They joined hands and Mary said her vows in French.

"I Mary, do accept Charles to be my husband and spouse …"

A gold ring was placed on her finger.

The court musicians played.

Mary was now to be known as Princess of Castile.

*

Following the ceremony there was a royal banquet. Mary danced with her brother and learned she would not be sent away to live with Charles as she was only thirteen. This, at least, was comforting news.

In the three days of celebrations that followed, Mary was presented with many gifts from her in-laws, including a letter from her new husband.

The letter was simple, easy to read.

It had been written by an eight-year-old boy.

It began: *Ma bonne compaigne …*

BASIL'S NIGHT WITH THE STARS
FRANCESCA MULVEY

1898, Rickinghall

Basil Brown woke with the sun one morning and wondered what to do once he had completed his chores on the farm. The cows needed milking, the eggs needed collecting from the hen house, and the horses' stalls needed mucking out, once the horses had been led out to graze.

"What about afterwards?" he said to himself.

Then a plan began to form in his thoughts.

Basil loved running round the untamed fields and wildflower meadows. There was a stream near his family's cottage and he would splash about in the water on warm days. This felt like a perfect idea.

But Basil also loved reading. He was now ten, so he was getting pretty good at it. Despite not being from a rich family, he had read several books. Over the spring, his parents had bought him a selection of second-hand copies with some of the money they had made from selling milk, eggs, and wool. Should he spend his free time reading one of these books?

With so many options, Basil decided to wait until after his chores were done to choose what he most wanted to do. So he pulled on his clothes and hurried down to the cow shed.

A few hours later, Basil was allowed to go and play.

"Don't go getting up to any mischief," his mother warned as she sat washing some of his clothes in the kitchen.

"I won't, Mum."

Free at last, Basil ran up the stairs to his bedroom and collapsed on the bed with a soft flump.

"I have so many things I want to do," he whispered, "but I can't decide what I really want to do …"

He stared at his bookshelf. His father had created it out of a few spare planks of strong wood leftover from repairing the horses' paddock. He had sanded them down using a pumice stone until it was soft to the touch.

On this shelf, Basil had placed the five books his mother and father had been kind enough to gift him for his birthday. A book of Hans Christian Andersen's fairy tales, a book about trees, A Study in Scarlet by Arthur Conan Doyle, an astronomy book, and a book on wildflowers, mushrooms, and fruits.

Basil's gaze returned to the astronomy book. Suddenly, he had an idea.

"I'll go play in the stream, run around the meadow, then I'll read my astronomy book."

And he knew just the place to do it. Up on the hill behind the cottage, where he would stay until his mother and father called him in for dinner and finally bed. But what they won't know, Basil thought to himself, is that I'll go back when it's dark …

With his newly formed plan fixed in his mind, he grabbed his astronomy book, threw it into the small leather satchel he kept by his door for adventures and headed out into the sunshine.

He splashed around in the stream for an hour or so, taking a break to have lunch with his mother and father, then playing in the nearby wildflower meadow. Often, he would lie down amongst the tall flowers and grasses to cool himself.

Afterwards, Basil ran up the hill behind the cottage and sat in his favourite spot against a large boulder buried in the earth. He often wondered about that boulder, how deep it went underground, and what sort of secrets lay hidden that neither rock nor soil would ever be able to tell.

He took out his astronomy book and began reading. There were pages upon pages about constellations, some of which had links to myths Basil had never heard of, and there were planets, far away from the earth.

His father came out of the barn after giving the pigs their evening feed.

"Son, inside for dinner!"

"Yes, Dad!"

*

Later, when it was dark and Basil felt sure his parents were asleep, he grabbed his bag along with his moleskin sketching journal and the secretly wrapped bread and cheese he had prepared for a late-night snack. Then he tip-toed downstairs.

He returned to his spot on the hill and sat under the light of the moon and the stars, staring up at them and sketching out the constellations. The plough, Orion, Regulus, just to name a few. They were dazzling.

Basil sat on that hill for hours, gazing up into the heavens.

"One day," he whispered, "I'm going to write a book of my own about the stars. And maybe I'll explore other things, too, like the secrets that lie hidden, somewhere far away."

And he gazed silently at the brightest star of them all, wondering where it would lead him, if he dared to follow.

TO SEE AND TO SPEAK
NATASHA O'BRIEN

1968, Ipswich

Jenny sat alone on the park bench enjoying the ice cream she had bought with her hard-earned pocket money. She looked around the park, up to the blue sky, and at the children playing on the swings. Then she saw someone familiar sitting on a nearby bench. It was the black man who had just moved into number four with his family.

Jenny's father had stood at the window shouting curses the day they had moved in. He told Jenny she wasn't to have anything to do with them. So when the man looked up at her, she quickly turned away and accidently dropped her ice cream. Jenny had just cleared away her mess when she heard a voice over her shoulder. She turned and saw the black man offering her a new ice cream.

"For you," he said.

Jenny bit her lip.

"I shouldn't accept treats from strangers."

He smiled. "That's true, but we ain't strangers, are we?"

Jenny nodded. There was something kind about him, so she smiled back.

"My name's Jenny."

"I'm Albert Grant."

"I guess we're friends now," she said, and thanked him for the ice cream.

Mr Grant sat down and opened his newspaper. Jenny recognised the man on the front page.

"Who's that?" she asked. "I've seen him on the telly."

Mr Grant looked at the picture.

"Oh, that's Mr Powell."

"My father thinks he's a hero. Do you?"

Mr Grant folded his paper. He took a deep, slow breath.

"No, can't say I do."

Jenny frowned. "How come?"

"There's only one thing Mr Powell has said that I agree with," said Mr Grant. "To see and not to speak, that is the great betrayal."

"What does it mean?"

"Depends who says it." Mr Grant leant forwards a little. "Words can have many meanings, you see. Mr Powell uses those words to make people angry and scared of each other. But when said by someone else – someone with a good heart – they could bring people together."

Jenny nodded. Then she saw her friends entering the park.

"I hope we meet again, Mr Grant."

She offered her hand and he shook it with a smile.

"I hope so too, Jenny."

Later that day, Jenny and her family were having dinner when they heard shouting in the street. They rushed into the front garden and saw two cars drive past number four, dumping rubbish on the grass and throwing bricks at the house.

Soon, all of the neighbours were gathered in their front gardens, watching the spectacle. Jenny's heart broke when she saw Mr Grant step outside carrying a brick that had broken through his window.

"Daddy," she said. "We should go help them."

Her father shook his head.

"Let him clean up his own mess."

He turned to go back inside but Jenny grabbed his arm. She pointed to Mr Grant's children.

"Daddy, look! They're the same age as me and they're frightened."

But her father only shrugged and turned again to the house.

Anger grew in Jenny's belly. She shouted, loud enough so all the neighbours could hear.

"To see and not speak, that is the great betrayal!"

Jenny's father stopped. He turned towards her, puzzled.

The low murmur of gossiping whispers was silenced. Jenny sensed that all eyes were now on her.

"Where did you hear that?" he asked.

"When you heard those words before, they made you afraid of people like Mr Grant," she told him. "But look at them. They're just like you and me! It doesn't matter where they come from or if they were born somewhere else. They're here, living and breathing just like you and me, and they have a heart that breaks when people are cruel to them, just like you and me!"

Jenny's father stood silent. She couldn't tell if the look on his face was shame or anger. Then he disappeared inside the house. She figured it must have been both.

Jenny walked over and helped to clear up the mess in Mr Grant's garden. The neighbours hovered close by, still whispering. Then they fell silent as Jenny's father walked through the front gate, carrying some plywood and his toolbox.

Without saying a word, he held up the board, covered the broken window, and started hammering it in place.

Jenny watched as Mr Grant stood upright and held his head high. Then he stepped forwards to help her father with the window.

The neighbours watched without any more gossip. Then one by one, they all joined to help.

Jenny smiled at Mr Grant. She realised that he had been right, that words could bring people together. All she needed was the courage to see and to speak.

THE PRINCE OF MANY FEATHERS
SOLOMON HOLMES

1925, Newmarket

George held his father's hand tightly as he led him through the manic traffic of suit-jacketed men and wide-hatted women standing at the races. The crowd was dressed so smartly that they moved like a sea of grey across the stadium's front plaza.

George was glad his father had made him wear his tweed waistcoat and smart black shoes. They were the only proper pieces of clothing he had, a hand-me-down from generations past. It didn't matter that they didn't quite fit him. It made him stand out less among the racing crowds. George didn't like to stand out, then.

There was one person among the crowd, however, who did stand out. The first thing George noticed were the Ostrich feathers. They were enormous! Some were bright green, some bright red, and they swayed in the wind atop a golden hued headdress. The feathers stood a good two feet above the crowd, and beneath them was a black man whose attire was just as extravagant as his headdress. He wore a glorious golden coat adorned with buttons and broaches that glistened in the summer sun. His trousers were scarlet and baggy, and they moved like a flag in the light breeze. A horseshoe dangled from an ornate necklace he wore around his neck. He held a rolled-up bit of paper in his hand, which he swooped round and round, gathering people's attention.

"I gotta horse! I gotta horse! I gotta horse to beat the favourite!"

His voice thundered with tremendous warmth. It towered above the general racket of the crowd and the surrounding masses were transfixed. Everybody stopped talking as the man in the ostrich feather hat continued.

"Why bet on the favourite? Eh? Everybody bet on the favourite. Why not stand out a little? I gotta tip that'll send you all home smiling!"

"Who's that, Dad?" asked George, prodding his father on the shoulder.

His father smiled warmly, crouched down and allowed George to climb on his back for a better view.

"That's the great Prince Monolulu. He's a horseracing tipster, and the luckiest around. Some say he used to be a tribal chief and a lion tamer in Abyssinia. You can sometimes see him wearing lion's paws and shark's teeth on his necklace as keepsakes from his past."

George stared open-mouthed at Prince Monolulu.

"His real name, or so I've heard, is Peter Carl Mckay. Some say he was shanghaied on board a British ship and that he called himself a prince to garner his fellow sailor's respect. Some say this same ship was shipwrecked along the Portuguese coast, and that Monolulu used this opportunity to escape to New York. Then he worked several jobs while he was there to pave his way to England for the 1903 Derby."

"What jobs did he work, Dad?" George was still transfixed on the seemingly fluorescent Prince Monolulu who continued to command the crowd.

"That's another matter for speculation, my boy! Some say he used to be a boxer, but you wouldn't believe it if his warm demeanour is anything to go by."

George listened closely as his father recounted how Prince Monolulu was also believed to have been a street dentist (it boggled George's mind to think how that would work), a fire eater in a circus, and a great entertainer.

"It's easy to see all that, isn't it, looking at him now."

George's jaw dropped open. His mind was aflame with images of Prince Monolulu's incredible past. He could see the tangible effect the man had on the crowd, almost as if an aura emanated from him and seeped into all those nearby, bringing joy.

"How do we know which of these stories are true?" he asked as the crowd followed Prince Monolulu into the stadium.

"Well, now," said his father, "I suppose we don't. But does that really matter? When I look at Prince Monolulu, I see a glorious self-made man, a natural born storyteller! I also see proof that there can be success in this world against adversity."

Prince Monolulu led the crowd to the stands. The race began, but no one was looking at the race. Instead, they were looking at the wonderful Prince Monolulu. George was looking, too, and just for a moment, the entertainer caught the boy's eye and gave him a wink. George grinned. In less than a flash, the entertainer disappeared behind his red and green feathers, but George would never forget the smile on his hero's face. He came back to the races at every opportunity, hoping to see the glorious Prince Monolulu once more, and his positive influence upon the world around him.